谷川俊太郎

詩集

佐野洋子

絵

集英社

女に　目次

- 未生 6
- 誕生 8
- こぶし 10
- 心臓 12
- 名 14
- 夜 16
- ふたり 18
- 素足 20
- かくれんぼ 22
- なめる 24
- 血 26
- 腕 28

- 谺 30
- 初めての 32
- 日々 34
- 日々また 36
- 会う 38
- 手紙 40
- 川 42
- 迷子 44
- 指先 46
- 唇 48
- ともに 50
- 電話 52

後生 76
死 74
夢 72
恍惚 70
笑う 68
墓 66
未来 64
蛇 62
旅 60
雑踏 58
ここ 56
…… 54

女に　谷川俊太郎詩集

未生

あなたがまだこの世にいなかったころ
私もまだこの世にいなかったけれど
私たちはいっしょに嗅いだ
曇り空を稲妻が走ったときの空気の匂いを
そして知ったのだ
いつか突然私たちの出会う日がくると
この世の何の変哲もない街角で

Before We Were Born

When you were yet unborn
and I was yet unborn,
we smelled together the scent of the air
when lightning sliced the cloudy sky.
And I realized that
some day suddenly we would meet
on an ordinary street corner here on earth.

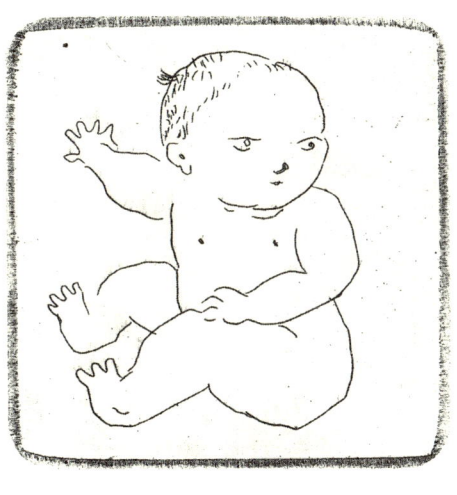

誕生

そのときも風が木々を渡ってきた
高利貸は指に唾つけて紙幣を数えていた
動物園でセイウチが吠えていた
そのときも世界は得体の知れぬものだった
あなたが暗くなまぐさい産道を
よじれながら光のほうへ進んできたとき

Birth

In that moment, too, the wind was blowing through the trees,
a usurer moistened his fingers and was counting bills,
and a walrus was barking in the zoo.
In that moment, too, the world was unknown to us
when you twisted and fought
through the birth canal, advancing toward the light.

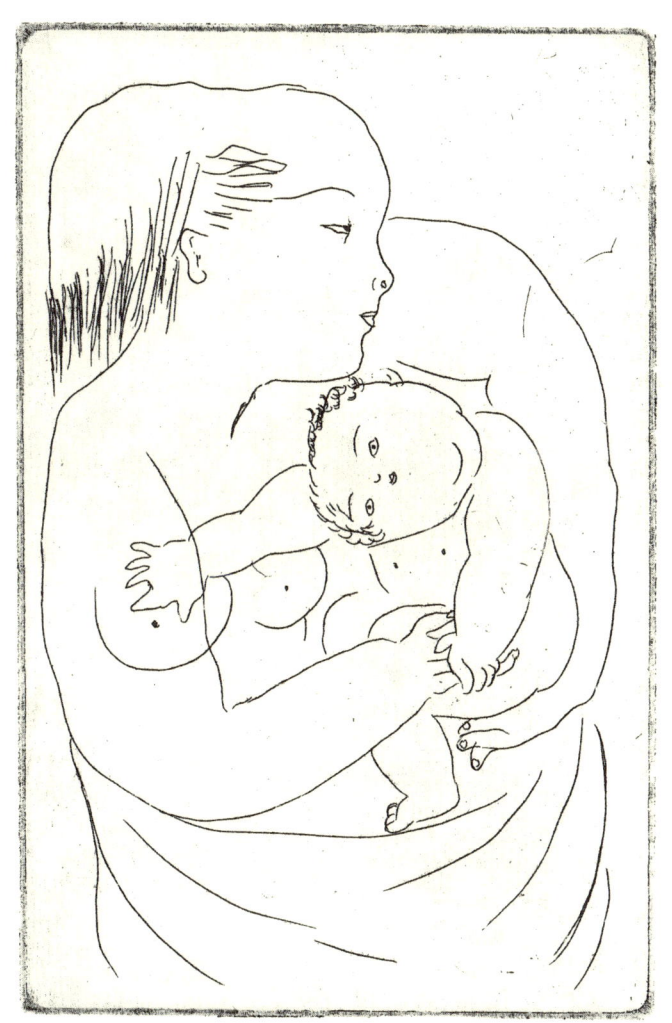

こぶし

なんだったの？
ちいさなちいさなこぶしの中に
固く握りしめていたものは
決してなくすまいとしていたものは
それをあなたは投げつける
まっすぐ私に向かって　いまも

A Fist

What was that
you clutched in your tiny, tiny fist,
clinging to it,
determined not to let loose of it?
You are flinging it straight at me,
even now.

心臓

それは小さなポンプにすぎないのだが
未来へと絶え間なく時を刻み始めた
それはワルツでもボレロでもなかったが
一拍ごとに私の喜びへと近づいてくる

Heart

It's merely a small pump but already
it's begun to tick off time, on and on, unceasingly, toward the future.
Not a waltz, not a bolero,
with each beat it draws nearer my joy.

名

誰も名づけることは出来ない
あなたの名はあなた
この世のすべてがほとばしり渦巻いて
あなたのやわらかいからだにそそぎこむ
幼い私の涙も溶け始めた氷河も

Name

No one can name you.
Your name is you.
The whole world gushes out
and, whirling, pours into your soft body —
even my infant tears and the melting glacier.

夜

兄さんと手をつないであなたは眠った
ひとり手を組んで私は眠った
夜の掛け布団の下で
あなたも私も敷布に夢の大陸を描き
朝になると見えない道を太陽にさらした

Night

You slept hand in hand with your brother.
I slept alone
with hands clasped beneath the quilt of night.
Dreaming, we both drew continents across the sheets
and in the morning spread out the unseen roads to the sun.

ふたり

影法師はどこまでもついてくる
でもついさっきまで遊んでいた子は
背をむけて行ってしまう
まわらぬ舌で初めてあなたが「ふたり」と数えたとき
私はもうあなたの夢の中に立っていた

We Two

Your shadow pursued you everywhere.
But your playmates of a moment ago
turned and went away.
When you lisped, "We're two", counting for the first time,
I was already standing in your dream.

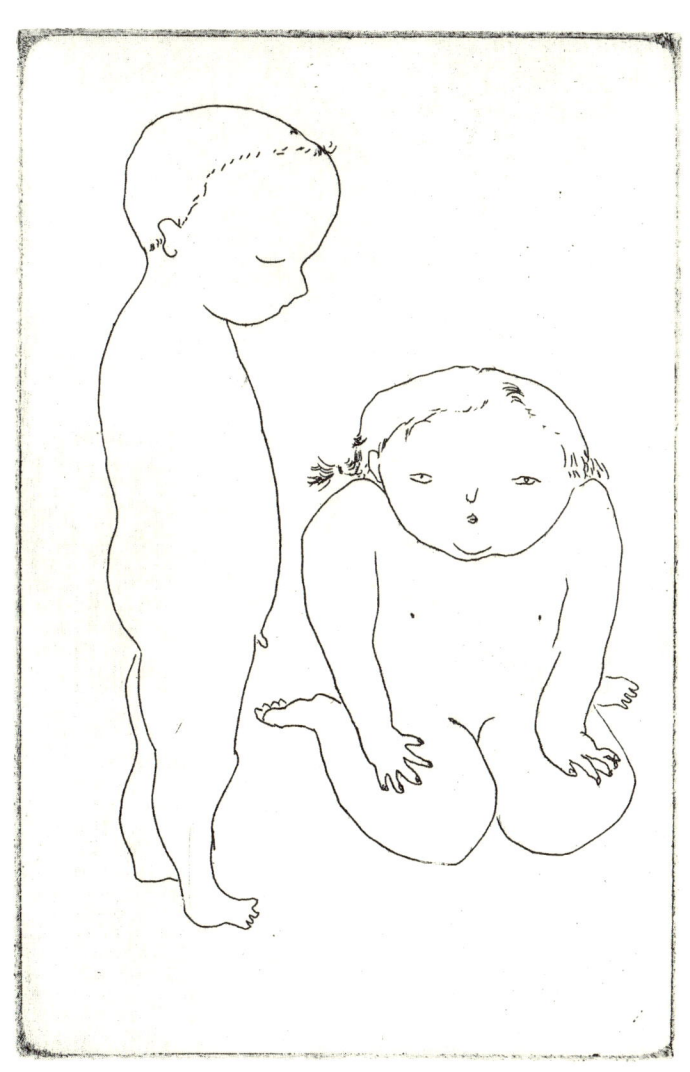

素足

赤いスカートをからげて夏の夕方
小さな流れを渡ったのを知っている
そのときのひなたくさいあなたを見たかった
と思う私の気持ちは
とり返しのつかない悔いのようだ

Barefooted

I know that you hiked up your red skirt
and waded across the shallow stream on a summer evening.
I wish I could have seen you then, smelling of sunlight.
I feel as if it's something
I could come close to regretting.

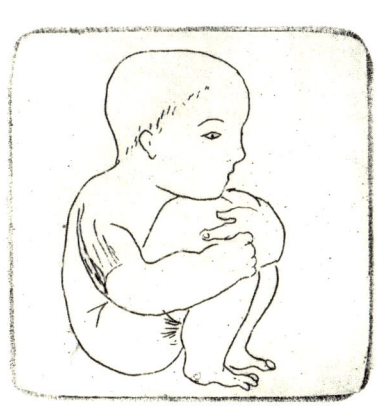

かくれんぼ

たった一本の立ち木が
あなたを私からかくしていた
「もういいよ」と叫ぼうとしてあなたはためらった
もっと待たねばならないと知っていたから
まだ目をつむって数えている私を

Hide and Seek

A single tree
hid you from me.
You were about to say, "I'm ready!", and then you hesitated.
You knew you would have to wait a little longer;
with my eyes closed I was still counting.

なめる

見るだけでは嗅ぐだけでは
聞くだけではさわるだけでは足りない
なめてあなたは愛する
たとえば一本の折れ曲がった古釘が
この世にあることの秘密を

Licking

Just seeing is not enough.
Nor just smelling, hearing or touching.
You lick and love something —
for example, the secret of an old bent nail
lying about here in this world.

血

星空と戦って
あなたが初めての血を流したとき
私は時の荒れ野に
種子を蒔くことをおぼえた
そうして私たちは死と和解するための
長い道のりの第一歩を踏み出した

Blood

When you disputed with the starry universe
and first shed your blood,
I learned to spread my seeds
on the wasteland of time.
And with these first steps, we set out
on our long journey toward reconciliation with death.

腕

あなたの腕の不思議な長さ
あなたの肩の匂うようななめらかさ
あなたの手の優雅なたけだけしさ
抱きしめるすべてに私がかくれていることを
あなたは知っていた

Arms

The surprising length of your arms,
the faint scent of your smooth shoulders,
the elegant audacity of your hand —
you knew that in everything that you embraced
I was hidden.

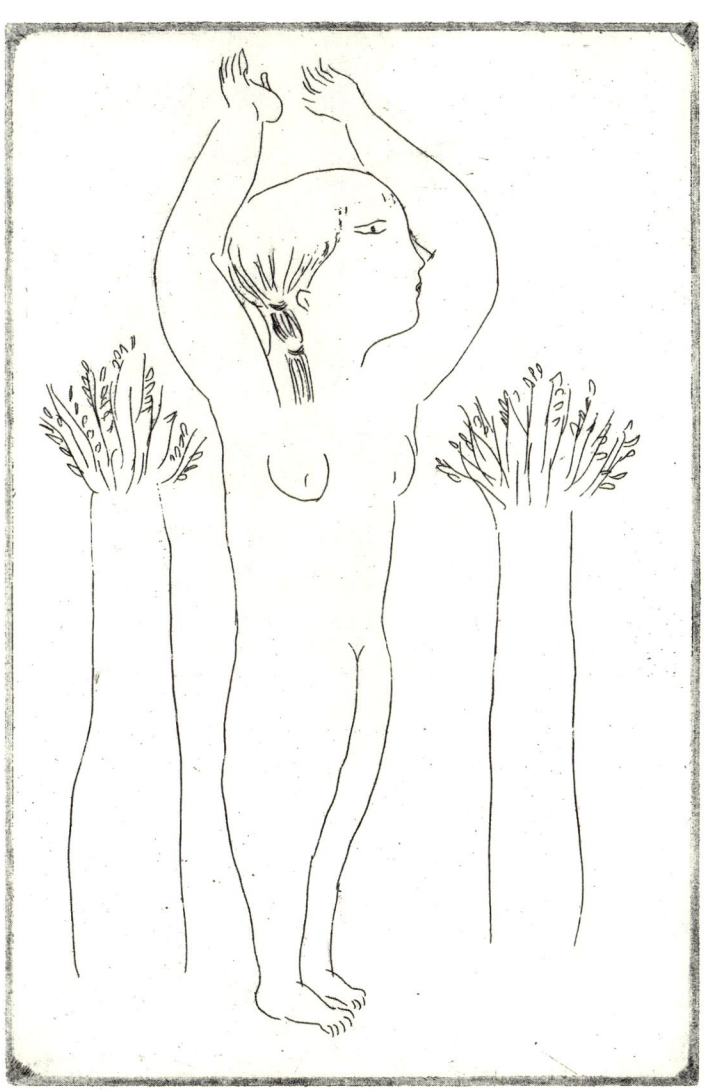

谺

声はまわり道をした
あなたを呼ぶ前に声は沈んでゆく夕陽を呼んだ
森を呼んだ　海を呼んだ　ひとの名を呼んだ
けれどいま私は知っている
戻ってきた谺はすべてあなたの声だったのだと

An Echo

My voice went roundabout.
It called the sinking sun before it called you.
It called the woods, the sea, people's names.
Yet now I know that every echo
was your voice.

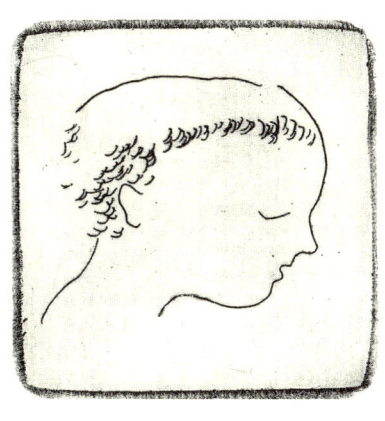

初めての
あなたの初めてのウィスキー
初めての接吻　初めての男
初めての異国の朝　初めての本物のボッシュ
しかもなおいつか私は初めての者として
あなたの前に立つだろう
その部屋の暗がりに　生まれたままの裸で

Your First

Your first whiskey,
your first kiss, your first lover,
your first morning in a foreign land,
your first look at a genuine Bosch....
even so, I will stand before you someday, your first man,
as naked as a newborn, in the room's darkness.

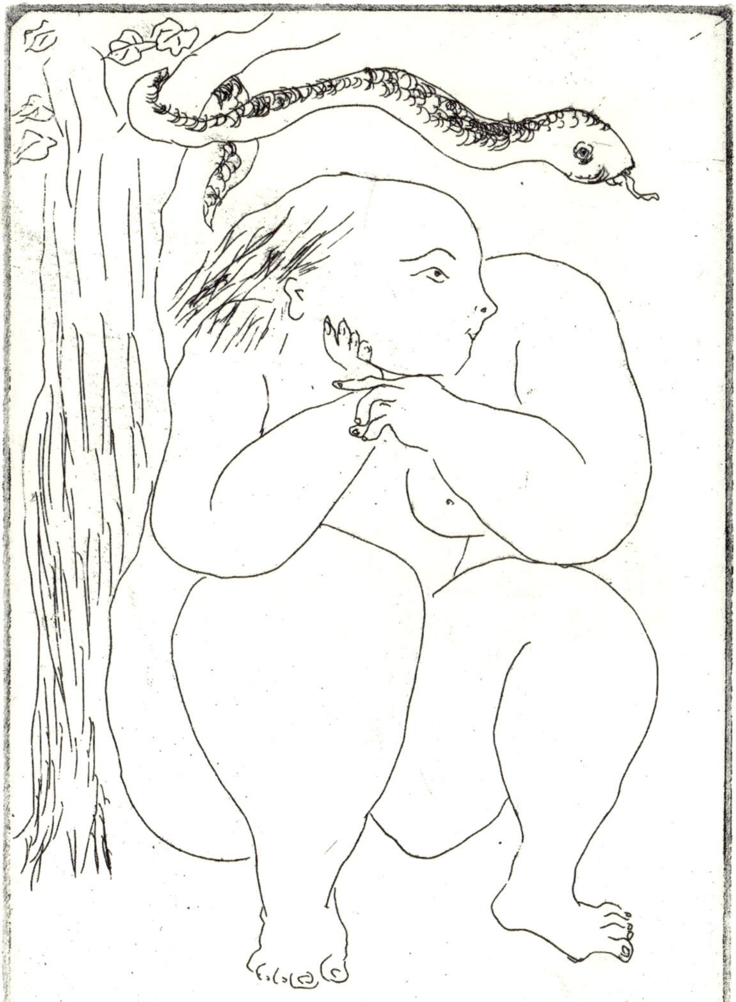

日々

私たちは別々の家で別々の物語を生きていた
雨だれが聞こえる朝　風が窓を鳴らす午後
その終わりがただひとつであることを知らずに
あなたの眠らなかった夜を私は眠ったが
私の知らないあなたの日々は
私の見た夕焼け雲に縁どられていた

Days

We were living separate stories in separate families,
through dripping morning rain and rattled windows,
unaware that both stories had but one ending.
I slept nights that you didn't sleep,
while your days that I knew nothing of
were fringed with the same evening glow that I saw.

日々また

あなたがお茶づけを食べている
あなたが息子に乳房をふくませる
あなたがバイクを始動する
あなたがひとりで涙を流している
私を知る前にあなたのしたことのひとつひとつ
……そのひとつひとつ

More Days

You were eating rice steeped in tea,
you were nursing your son,
your were starting up your motorcycle,
you were crying alone.
Each one of those things that you did before you knew me
....each and every one....

会う

始まりは一冊の絵本とぼやけた写真
やがてある日ふたつの大きな目と
そっけないこんにちは
それからのびのびしたペン書きの文字
私は少しずつあなたに会っていった
あなたの手に触れる前に
魂に触れた

Meeting

It all started with one picture book and a blurred snapshot.
Then one day your two large eyes
and a curt "Hello!"
And the free flow of your handwriting.
I encountered you bit by bit.
I touched your soul
before I touched your hand.

手紙

三千円の頭金で新車を買った
ワニ皮ベルトの不動産屋にだまされた
赤い塀の牢屋に入れられる夢を見た
あなたが日々の平凡な事実を
お伽話にしてしまうので
私は王子に生まれ変わる

A Letter

You paid three thousand yen down for a new car.
A realtor sporting a crocodile-skin belt cheated you.
You dreamed you were jailed inside of red walls.
Because you change the ordinary facts
of your daily life into a fairy tale,
I am reborn as a prince.

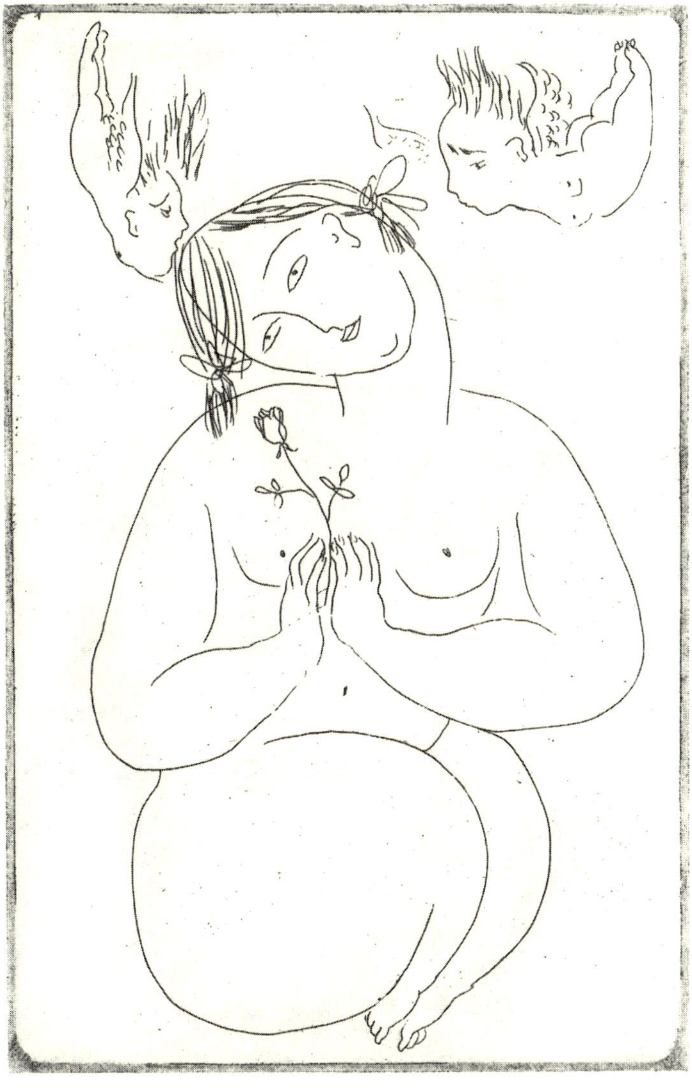

川

マンガを買って私はあなたと笑いにいく
西瓜を貰って私はあなたと食べにいく
詩を書いて私はあなたに見せにいく
何もたたずに私はあなたとぼんやりしにいく
川を渡って私はあなたに会いにいく

A River

I go to see you with a comic book so we can laugh together.
I go to see you with a watermelon so we can eat it together.
I go to see you with a poem I wrote.
I go to see you empty-handed, just so we can sit around together.
I go across the river to see you.

迷子

私が迷子になったらあなたが手をひいてくれる
あなたが迷子になったら私も地図を捨てる
私が気取ったらあなたが笑いとばしてくれる
あなたが老眼鏡を忘れたら私のを貸してあげる
そして私は目をつむり頭をあなたの膝にあずける

Getting Lost

If I get lost you'll lead me by the hand.
If you get lost I'll throw my map away.
If I become affected you'll dismiss me with laughter.
If you forget your bifocals I'll lend you mine,
and I'll close my eyes and rest my head on your lap.

指先

指先はなおも冒険をやめない
ドン・キホーテのように
おなかの平野をおへその盆地まで遠征し
森林限界を越えて火口へと突き進む

Fingertips

My fingertips keep venturing forth,
like Don Quixote, across the field of your belly
as far down as the basin of your navel, and below
the timberline, and plunge into the crater.

唇

笑いながら出来るなんて知らなかった
とあなたは言う
唇はとても忙しい
乳房と腿のあいだを行ったり来たり
その合間に言葉を発したりもするのだから

Lips

You say you didn't know
we could do this while laughing.
My lips are very busy travelling back and forth
between your breasts and thighs,
and saying things in between.

ともに

ともに生きるのが喜びだから
ともに老いるのも喜びだ
ともに老いるのが喜びなら
ともに死ぬのも喜びだろう
その幸運に恵まれぬかもしれないという不安に
夜ごと責めさいなまれながらも

Two Together

Because we live together joyfully,
growing old together is joyful.
If growing old together is joyful
so could dying together be.
And I am tormented every night by the fear that
our luck might not be that good.

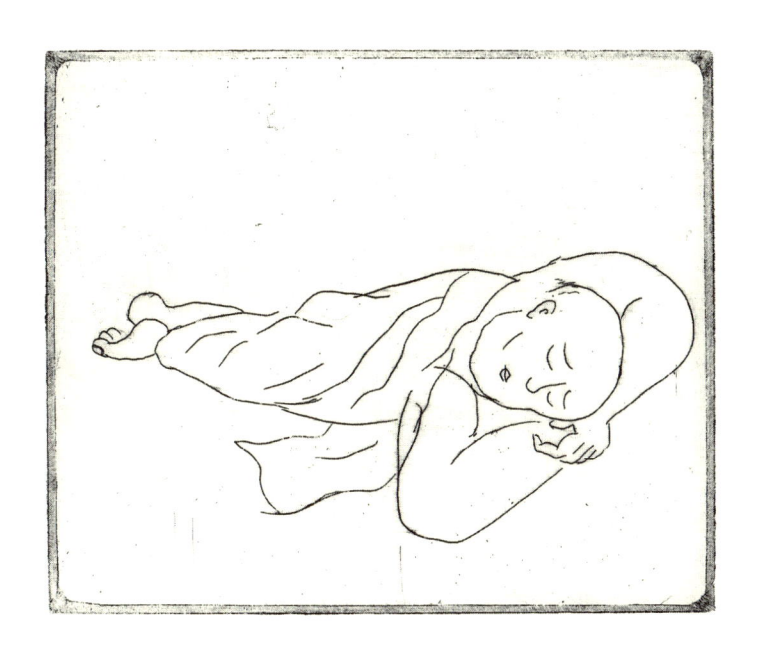

電話

あなたが黙りこんでしまうと時が凝固する
あなたの息の音にまじって
遠くで他人の笑い声が聞こえる
電話線を命綱に私は漂っている
もしあなたが切ったら……
もうどこにも戻れない

A Telephone

When you fall silent, time freezes.
Under your breath I hear
distant laughter mixed in.
I am adrift, the telephone wire my lifeline.
If you hang up....
I have nowhere to go back to.

　　　　　　　　　　　　　……

砂に血を吸うにまかせ
死んでゆく兵士たちがいて
ここでこうして私たちは抱きあう
たとえ今めくるめく光に灼かれ
一瞬にして白骨になろうとも悔いはない
正義からこんなに遠く私たちは愛しあう

…..

Even now as soldiers bleed
on the sand and die,
we are here in this embrace.
I wouldn't regret it, even if we were seared by a blinding light,
and our bones were bleached instantly white.
So far away from Justice, we make love.

ここ

どっかに行こうと私が言う
どこ行こうかとあなたが言う
ここもいいなと私が言う
ここでもいいねとあなたが言う
言ってるうちに日が暮れて
ここがどこかになっていく

Here

I say, "Let's go somewhere."
You say, "Where to?"
"Here is good enough," I say.
"It's all right with me, too," you say.
While we are talking, the day ends
and this place is now some other place.

雑踏

幻が私たちをみつめている
大きな澄みきった目で
だからこんなにもはっきりと分かるのだ
枝々があなたの乳房をつかみ
川が私の腿に流れこむのが
この夕暮れの市場の雑踏の只中でさえ

A Crowd

A vision is watching us
with eyes so large and clear
that I can distinctly make out
branches grasping your breasts
and the river flowing into my thighs,
even here in the midst of this bustling market.

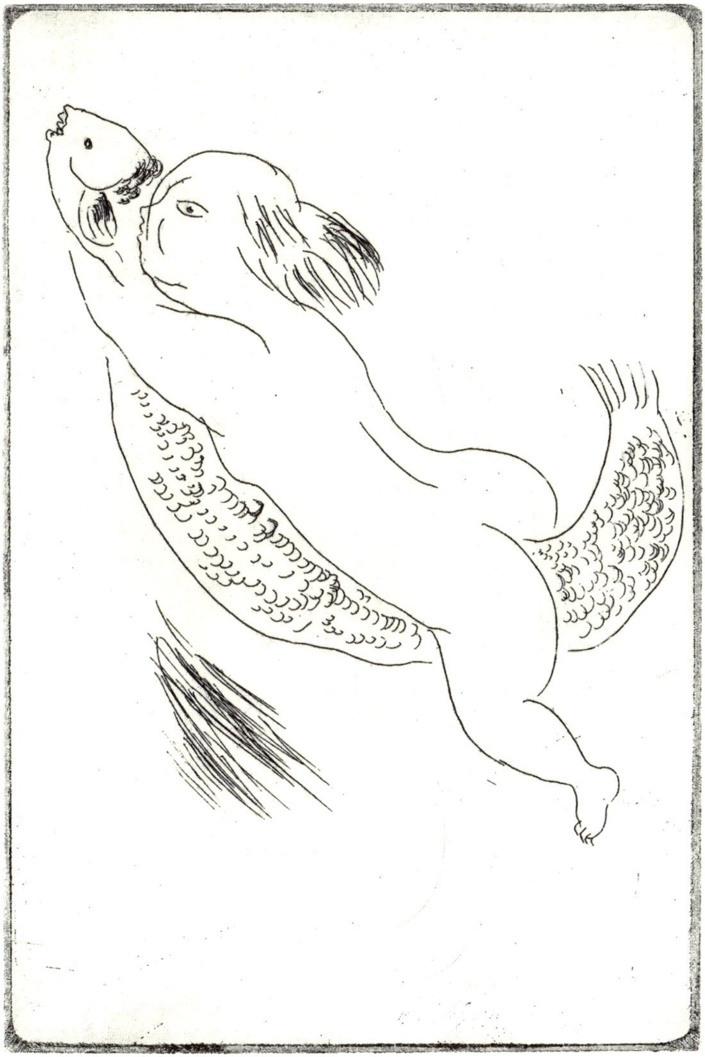

旅

修道院の前庭のオリーヴの木陰で
あなたは本を読んでいる
まるで自分の家にいるようにくつろいで
白昼の風景に溶けこむあなたの静けさ
そこから影のようにひとつの言葉が生まれ……
あなたは私にむかって顔をあげる

A Journey

You are reading a book beneath an olive tree
in this monastery garden,
as if you were at home.
Your quietness merges with midday,
and out of that quietness a word is born like a shadow....
and you lift your face to me.

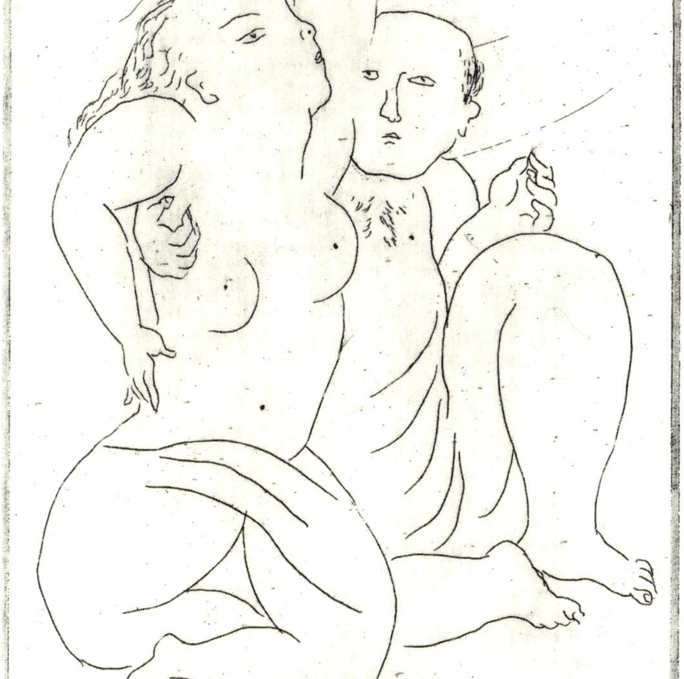

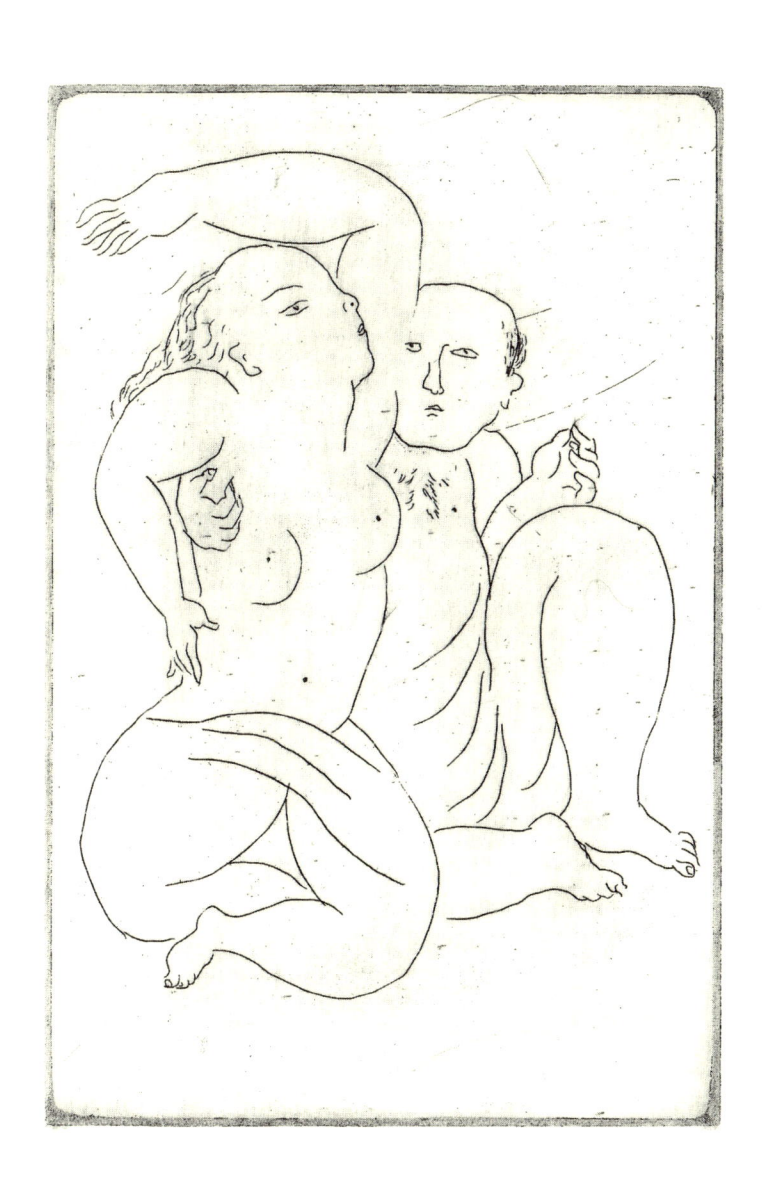

蛇

あなたが私のしっぽを呑みこみ
私があなたのしっぽに食らいつき
私たちは輪になった二匹の蛇　身動きができない
輪の中に何を閉じこめたのかも知らぬまま

Snakes

You swallow my tail,
and I snap at yours.
We are two snakes forming an unbreakable ring.
What we have ringed in, we don't know.

未来

たった今死んでいいと思うのにまだ未来がある
あなたが問いつめ私が絶句する未来
原っぱでおむすびをぱくつく未来
大声で笑いあったことを思い出す未来
もう何も欲しいとは思わないのに
まだあなたが欲しい

Future

Though I wouldn't mind dying at this moment, still there are
 futures —
the future you press me about, and I can't answer;
the future when we will eat rice balls on the field;
the future when we will recall having laughed aloud.
Though there's no longer anything I want,
I want you.

墓

汗びっしょりになって斜面を上った
草の匂いに息がつまった
そこにその無骨な岩はあった
私たちは岩に腰かけて海を見た
やがて私たちは岩を冠に愛しあうだろう
土のからだで　泥の目で　水の舌で

A Grave

Climbing the slope, we sweat profusely;
choked on the acrid odor of the weeds.
We came across a jagged rock,
sat on it and looked down at the sea.
Before long we shall be in love beneath this rock-crown,
our bodies earth, our eyes mud, our tongues water.

笑う

私たちは笑う
老いた者の仮借なさで笑う
寝そべってライチをむきながら笑う
腰の痛みに顔をしかめて笑う
平凡を笑う　非凡を笑う
歯のない口で笑う

We Laugh

We laugh.
With the relentlessness of old people, we laugh.
Lying about, peeling lichees, we laugh.
Grimacing at the pain in our backs, we laugh.
At the ordinary, at the extraordinary, we laugh.
Toothless, we laugh.

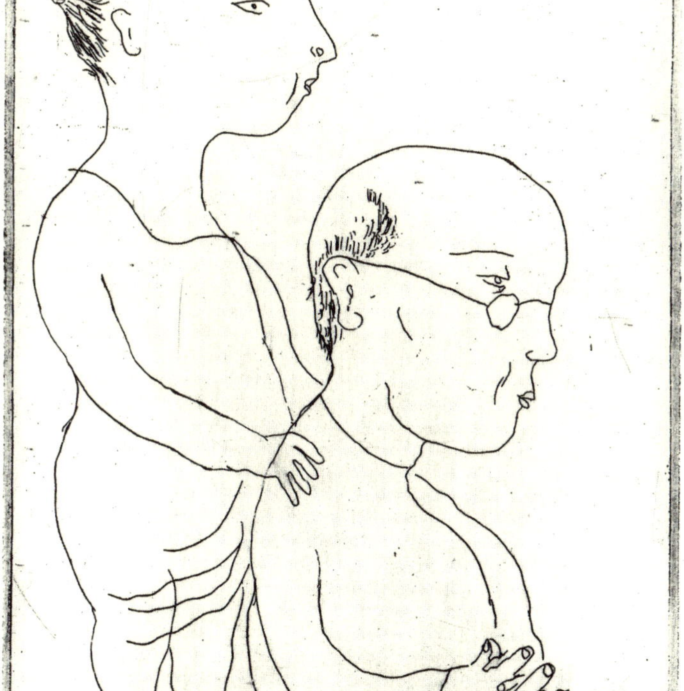

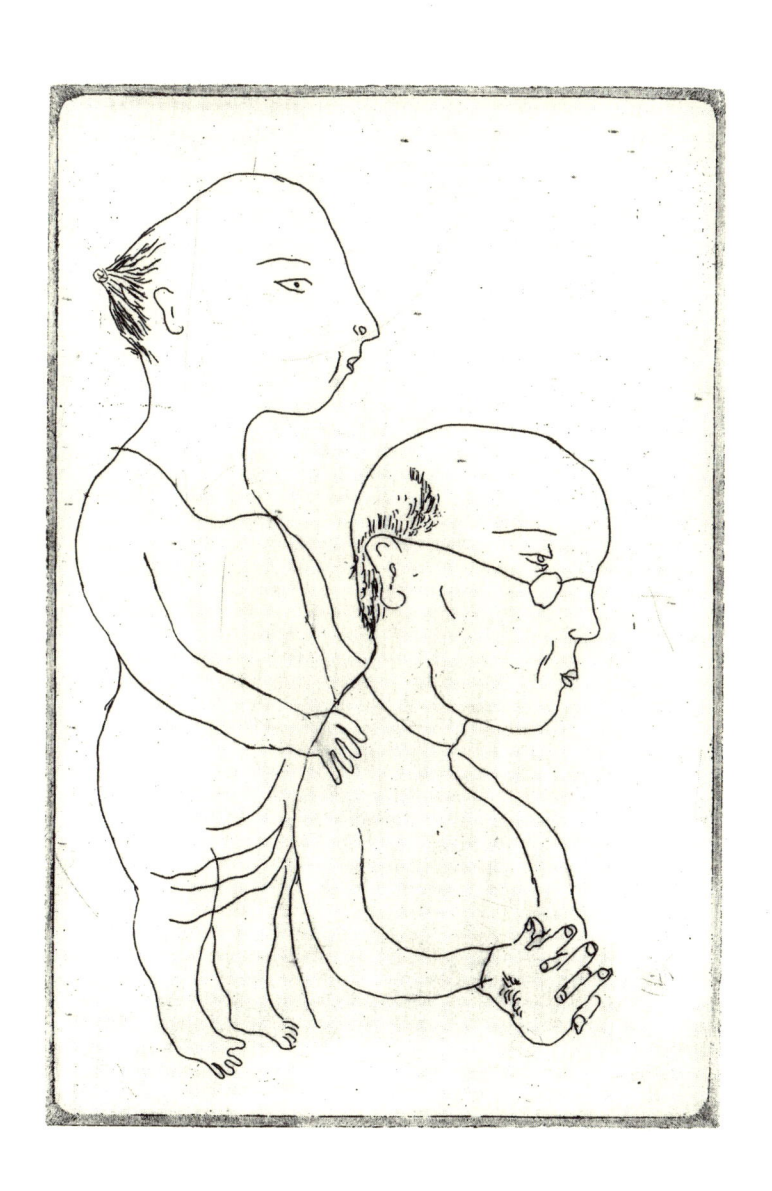

恍惚

おむつ代えるついでに
あなたは私の尻をつねってくれる
隣の寝たきりばあさんが美人だからだ
私の脳細胞は恍惚として目覚めるだろう
知性の遠く及ばぬものに

Entranced

When you change my diapers
you jealously pinch my buttocks,
because of the "beautiful" old woman in the next bed.
My brain cells will waken, entranced,
to something far beyond mere intellect.

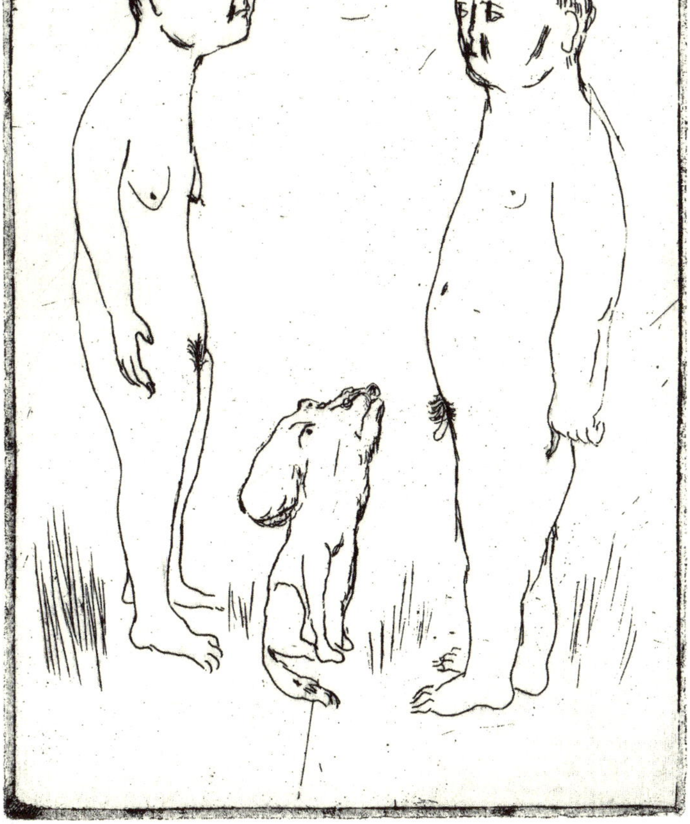

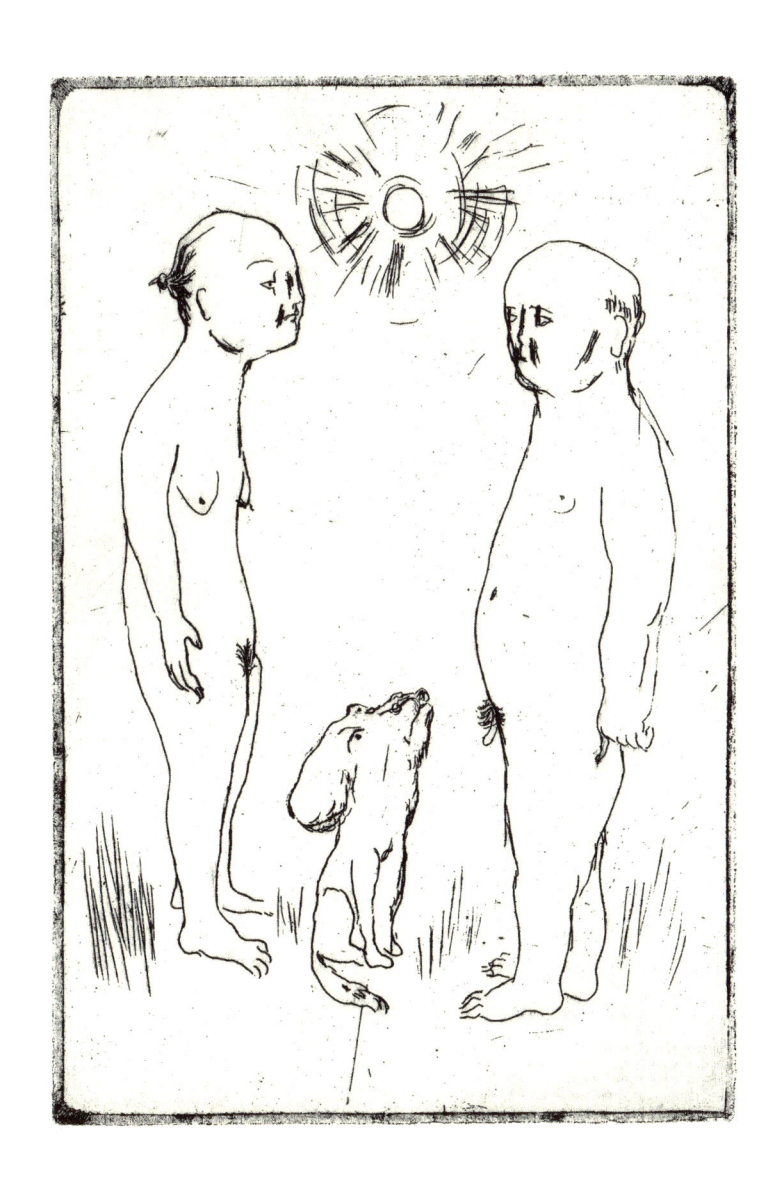

夢

金いろの赤ん坊がふたり
青空の下で金いろのうんこをしている
あなたの描く絵の中に私たちはいる
しっかりと手を握りあって
時が無力になるほうへよちよち歩いてゆく

A Dream

Two golden babies are pooping
golden poop beneath the blue sky.
We are in the picture you draw.
Hand in hand, we lurch
towards a place where time is impotent.

死

私ハ火ニナッタ
燃エナガラ私ハアナタヲミツメル
私ノ骨ハ白ク軽ク
アナタノ舌ノ上デ溶ケルダロウ
麻薬ノヨウニ

Death

I have become fire.
Burning, I watch you.
My bones, white and light,
will melt away on your tongue
like a narcotic.

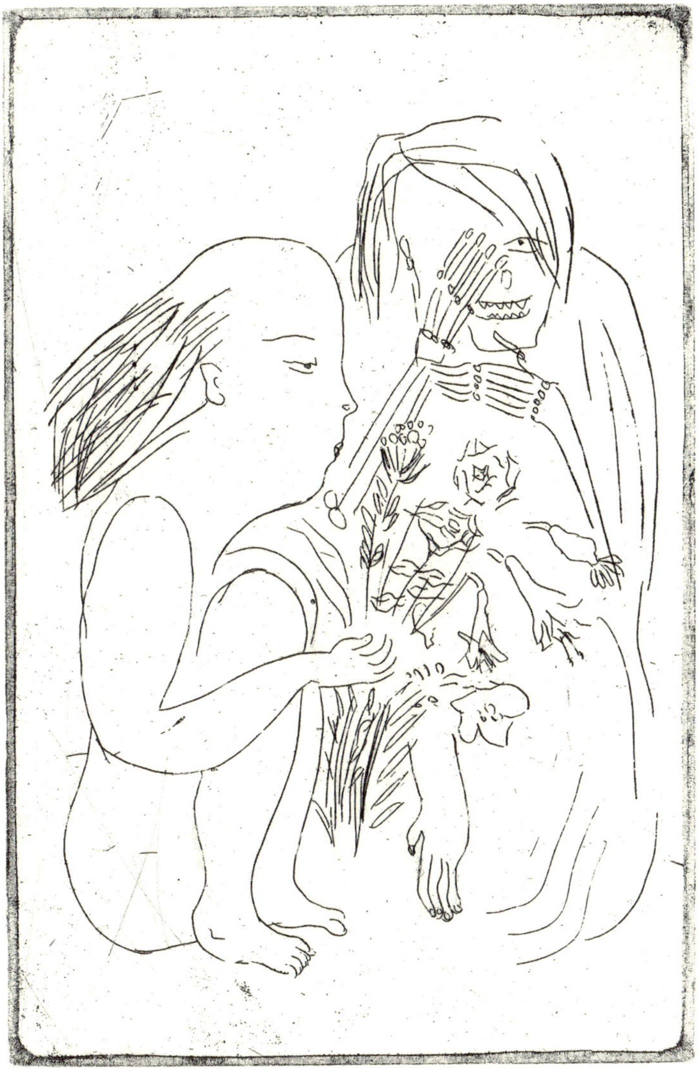

後生

きりのないふたつの旋律のようにからみあって
私たちは虚空とたわむれる
気まぐれにつけた日記　並んで眠った寝台
訪れた廃墟と荒野　はき古した揃いの靴
地上に残した僅かなものを懐かしみながら

After We Die

Intertwined like two endless tunes,
we play around with empty space,
fondly recalling a few things we left behind on earth —
the diary we kept at random, the bed we slept in,
ruins and wildernesses visited, two pairs of identical shoes
　worn out together.

本書は、一九九一年三月にマガジンハウスより刊行された『女に』を底本とし、新たに英語訳を付したものです。

装丁・本文レイアウト──平野甲賀
英訳──W・I・エリオット／川村和夫

女に

二〇一二年十二月一〇日　第一刷発行
二〇二三年　九月一八日　第二刷発行

著者——谷川俊太郎（たにかわしゅんたろう）
装画——佐野洋子（さのようこ）
発行者——樋口尚也
発行所——株式会社集英社
　　　　東京都千代田区一ツ橋二—五—一〇　〒一〇一—八〇五〇
　　電話　〇三—三二三〇—六一〇〇（編集部）
　　　　　〇三—三二三〇—六三九三（販売部）書店専用
　　　　　〇三—三二三〇—六〇八〇（読者係）
印刷所——大日本印刷株式会社
製本所——加藤製本株式会社

©2012 Tanikawa Shuntaro & JIROCHO, Inc. Printed in Japan
ISBN978-4-08-771476-0　C0092

定価はカバーに表示してあります。
造本には十分注意しておりますが、印刷・製本など製造上の不備がありましたら、お手数ですが小社「読者係」までご連絡下さい。古書店、フリマアプリ、オークションサイト等で入手されたものは対応いたしかねますのでご了承下さい。
本書の一部あるいは全部を無断で複写・複製することは、法律で認められた場合を除き、著作権の侵害となります。また、業者など、読者本人以外による本書のデジタル化は、いかなる場合でも一切認められませんのでご注意下さい。